To my daughter, Lena, and our friend Julian, who first listened to this story sitting on my lap, patiently waiting for the subway to Coney Island. And to Julie, who, after seventeen years of marriage, I still believe is the single grapest girl in the world —A.M.

For Pia, Isabel, and Kier — G.P.

Text copyright © 2007 by Alan Madison
Illustrations copyright © 2007 by Giselle Potter

Published in the United States by Schwartz & Wade Books, an imprint of Random House Children's Books, a division of Random House, Inc., New York.

Schwartz & Wade Books and colophon are trademarks of Random House, Inc.

www.randomhouse.com/kids
Educators and librarians, for a variety of teaching tools, visit us at www.randomhouse.com/teachers

Library of Congress Cataloging-in-Publication Data

Madison, Alan.
The littlest grape stomper / by Alan Madison ; illustrated by Giselle Potter. — 1st ed.
p. cm.
Summary: Having twelve toes has always caused problems for young Sixto, but especially when Boss Nova Boombatz lures him into the town of Ear's business of making grape juice when he would rather just play.
ISBN 978-0-375-83675-6 (hardcover) — ISBN 978-0-375-93675-3 (lib. bdg.)
[1. Toes—Fiction. 2. Grape juice—Fiction. 3. Humorous stories. 4. Tall tales.] I. Potter, Giselle, ill. II. Title.

PZ7.M2587Li 2007
[Fic]—dc22
2006003832

The text of this book is set in Packard.
The illustrations are rendered in pencil, ink, gouache, gesso, and watercolor.
Book design by Lee Wade and Anne Schwartz

PRINTED IN CHINA

1 3 5 7 9 10 8 6 4 2

First Edition

# the Littlest Grape Stomper

Written by Alan Madison

Illustrated by Giselle Potter

Schwartz & Wade Books · New York

The tiny village of Ear, nestled snugly in the Your Valley, was known for doing one thing extremely well: making scrumptious grape juice.

Every hill and dale near Ear was covered in vines loaded with perfectly plump grapes. And each simmering summer, all the men and women picked these round lovelies and stomped them into the famed purpley lip-smacking liquid.

In the inner part of Ear, there lived a boy
named Sixto Poblano. He was named Sixto
because when he was born there were six little
newborn toes on each of his little newborn feet.

Every morning Sixto
would count,
"One,
two,
three,
four,
five . . ."

And there they
always were,
sprouting from
the side of
each foot like
bent broccolis.
His sixth toes.

Sixto did not at all appreciate having this extra bit of footage. At the shoe store there was never a good fit, and when he ran he often tripped.

But having six toes was not all bad, all the time. In kickball Sixto was always chosen first because when he put foot to ball, it flew!

One day on his way to work, Boss Nova Boombatz, the big head of all things grape, stumbled upon the children playing. Hands on hips, he watched Sixto boom kick after kick over the fence.

An inkling of an idea snaked into old Boombatz's nasty nottled noggin.

"A boy like you could help us at harvest," he said smoothly.

"I'd rather play, sir," replied young Sixto politely.

The Boss circled his multi-muscled arm over Sixto's shoulder and sweet-syruped his voice. "Indeed you would. Who wouldn't? But we in Ear pick, pluck, and stomp—that is our sworn duty. And you, me boy, clearly have talent."

Sixto lapped up the sugared words and followed Boombatz into the fields.

The boy watched the villagers pick and pluck the plump purple clusters off the vines. When their baskets were full, they poured the ripe rounds into wooden barrels.

Next, the stompers stepped in and started stomping.

Sixto carefully climbed into his big barrel. He stomped once, then twice, squishing and squashing every grape into grape juice.

The other stompers stopped stomping and
stared in eye-popping, jaw-dropping astonishment.
"What's the problem here?" Boss Boombatz
blustered.
"Sixto! He stomped just twice!" they crowed.
"Show me," Boombatz demanded.

And Sixto did. He clambered into another barrel, stomped once, then twice, and because his spare toes made his feet so worldly wide, all the juicy grapes were now grape juicy.

Boombatz popped the cork at the base of the barrel, filled the dented tin cup that dangled from his belt, and slurped.

"Deeeliciousss!" he proclaimed, adding extra *ee*'s and *ss*'s for emphasis.

You see, no one in Ear had done anything like this before. Twelve stomps at least, ten stomps sometimes, eight stomps once, but *two* stomps? Unheard of! Here was a barrel-squishing feat fit for the *Boombatzy Book of Your Valley Records*.

Suddenly, the bloquacious Boombatz was struck with a thunderous brainstorm. . . .

That night, from dusk until dawn, the sounds of *bim-bam* hammering and *seesaw* sawing rolled down the hillside.

And when Sixto arrived for work the next morning, where the bulky barrel had once sat, there now stood a titanic tub!

Day after day all picked, plucked, and poured until the tub overflowed.

"Ready?" asked Boss Nova Boombatz.

"I'd rather play, sir," Sixto innocently answered.

The Boss tightly circled his multi-muscled arm over Sixto's slight shoulder.

"Listen here, you. We in Ear pick, pluck, and stomp—that, me boy, is our job."

Now the words that dribbled out from deep in Boss Nova's throat sounded less like sweet syrup and more like thick gravy.

Sixto counted, "One, two, three, four, five." Then, wiggling the wide wonders that sprouted off each side, "Six," he called. "I'm ready." And he tugged off his clothes, climbed the ladder . . .

. . . and leapt in!

His thick thighs lifting, his dozen digits
squishing, he stomped and stomped.

As the sun dripped behind the hills, the empurpled Sixto hoisted himself out. Boombatz unplugged the cork, filled his metal mug, and gulped. "Deeeliciousss!" he proclaimed, amazed because this had certainly never been done before—a whole week's grapes crushed in one single day.

This accomplishment was of such magnitude that Sixto was now eligible for entry into the Grape Juicing Hall of Fame.

The Earians rejoiced. They lifted the purplescent boy on their shoulders and carried him through the town. As they paraded past, Sixto's friends stopped their playing to wave.

Week after summer week, the titanic tub was filled, and day after hot day, Sixto stomped away. Each evening when he headed home, his friends would ask him to play, but he was always too tired.

After a while they stopped asking.

So although Sixto was listed in the *Boombatzy Book of Your Valley Records* and enshrined in the Grape Juicing Hall of Fame, he was lonely.

Sixto was sure Boombatz could fix this small problem, so one evening he marched straight up to the Boss and interrupted his sumptuous supper.

"Hungry, me boy?" asked Boombatz, looking up from his piled-high platter.

"I miss my friends," stated Sixto plainly.

The Boss swallowed hard, nearly choking on his chowder.

"My talented tot," he cooed sweetly, grabbing hold of Sixto's hand, "you have found your future, and it is at the bottom of my barrels."

Head hung low, Sixto turned and started away.

A growl began to grow in Boombatz's chest. But just as he was about to bark at the boy, he got smacked silly with a particularly perfect plan.

He flashed his most toothsome smile. "All I ask is one last goodbye mushing," he called.

Sixto stopped in his tracks. "That seems fair."

"Fair is fair," repeated the Boss, sealing the deal with a fiendishly phony handshake.

That night, all the ears of Ear were filled with the furious *bim-bam* of hammers, the frantic *seesaw* of saws, and the frenzied *scree-scraw* of screwdrivers.

At sunrise, looming over the town, exactly where the big barrel had sat, precisely where the titanic tub had towered, there now stood the most colossal container ever constructed.

With every Earian—young and old, big and small—picking, it took forty days to gather enough grapes to fill the container. At last it was Sixto's turn to churn. He climbed to the top, winked, waved, and dove in. He stomped once, twice, then stomped and stomped and stomped.

The village orchestra came to play. Sixto did a jig as
the sun tumbled and did a polka as the moon rumbled up.
Mighty thighs purple-pumping, all twelve toes squish-squashing,
he slogged through the sludge for seven days and nights, until the
gigantic juicing was done.

BAND of EAR

But when Sixto tried to get out of the container, he could not! He had crushed the plump bunches so completely that he was far from the top. And no matter how he stretched and shimmied, joggled and juked, he just couldn't reach the rim.

"Help!"

Sixto's yell bounced off the walls.

"Help! *Help!* HELP!" he triple-howled, but outside, the orchestra played on, drowning his pleas. Tired from treading, Sixto started to sink, then sank, and finally sunk.

From the bottom of the barrel, Sixto heard Boss Boombatz's muffled voice—

"Deeeliciousss."

And turning just in time to see the massive cork being pushed back into place, Sixto got an idea of his own. With his last breath, he bent his beefy legs and blasted a mighty kick.

The cork went flying!
The violet liquid exploded out!
"My tasty juice," cried Boombatz as it gushed, "ruined! RUINED!"

Like a raging river it swept up everything in its gigantic juician path; the Boombatz, the pickers, the stompers, and all of Sixto's friends.

And there atop the crest of this grand grape tidal wave, calmly riding on his surfboard-wide feet, was Sixto Poblano.

At last the container emptied and
the fruity flood stopped, dropping the Earians
on a far hill. The Your Valley and all the other
nearby valleys were completely covered with the
deep dark juice. And that is how, a very long time ago,
the five Grape Lakes were formed.

The Earians built their new village there, and
the children returned to their playing.
Sixto still had trouble getting
shoes, still tripped when
he ran, and was still chosen
first for kickball. But now all
those firsts are fine by him,
because he truly appreciates the
importance of being two toes different.

And what of old Boss Nova Boombatz? Well, he was never heard from again. Legend has it that he remained under juice, forever swimming the five Grape Lakes, traveling from Huron to Ontario to Michigan to Erie to Superior, sipping and slurping the "deeeliciousss" drink he loved most.